The Case of the Runaway Turtle

Book created by Parker C. Hinter

Written by Della Rowland

Illustrated by Chuck Slack

Based on characters from the Parker Brothers game

A Creative Media Applications Production

SCHOLASTIC INC.
New York Toronto London Auckland Sydney

065×9100891654/3

No part of this publication may be reproduced in whole or in part, or stored in a retrieval system, or transmitted in any form or by any means, electronic, mechanical, photocopying, recording, or otherwise, without written permission of the publisher. For information regarding permission, write to Scholastic Inc., 555 Broadway, New York, NY 10012.

ISBN 0-590-62373-7

12 11 10 9 8 7 6 5 4 3 2 1   6 7 8 9/9 0 1/0

Printed in the U.S.A.   40

First Scholastic printing, June 1996

Contents

Contents

The Case of the Runaway Turtle

Introduction

Meet the members of the Clue Club.

Samantha Scarlet, Peter Plum, Georgie Green, Wendy White, Mortimer Mustard, and Polly Peacock.

These young detectives are all in the same fourth-grade class. The thing they have most in common, though, is their love of mysteries. They formed the Clue Club to talk about mystery books they have read, mystery TV shows and movies they like to watch, and also, to play their favorite game, Clue Jr.

These mystery fans are pretty sharp when it comes to solving real-life mysteries, too. They all use their wits and deductive skills to crack the cases in this book.

You can match *your* wits with this gang of junior detectives to solve the eight mysteries. Can you guess who did it? Check the solution that appears upside down after each story to see if you were right!

The Case of the Soccer Sweatshirt

Polly Peacock, Wendy White, Peter Plum, Mortimer Mustard, and Georgie Green were sitting in the school lunchroom finishing up their lunch. "Where's Samantha?" Polly asked the others. "She's going to miss lunch period if she doesn't get here soon."

Just then, Samantha Scarlet ran through the lunchroom door. She grabbed a chair and plopped down with the rest of the Clue Club kids. "Today's the day!" she panted.

"For what?" asked Peter.

"Today's the day I find out," Samantha said.

"Find out *what*?" asked Polly.

"If I made the soccer team," said Samantha, smiling. She closed her eyes and crossed her fingers. "Hope, hope, hope," she said.

Earlier that month, Samantha had tried out for the junior soccer team for fourth-, fifth-, and sixth-graders. If she made it, she would be the only girl on the team.

"That's why I'm late for lunch," Samantha explained. "I went to Coach Green's office."

"What did the coach tell you?" asked Peter.

"He said he was having a hard time deciding," Samantha answered. "A lot of good kids tried out. Anyway, he's going to post the names of the team outside his office after school."

"Well, you better hurry up and eat your lunch," said Wendy. "Lunch period is going to be over soon."

Samantha opened her bag and took out a sandwich and a chocolate cupcake. "I don't know if I can eat my lunch," she said. "I'm too excited."

"Well, if you don't want that cupcake, I'll be glad to eat it," said Mortimer. "I wouldn't want it to get stale."

"Eating is Mortimer's sport," laughed Polly.

"Eating is most excellent," said Mortimer. "It's the best way to keep your jaws exercised, you know."

Just then the lunch bell rang. "Only three more classes until you know if you're on the team, Samantha," said Peter. "Good luck."

After school, Samantha and the other kids raced to the soccer coach's office. Several boys were crowded around the office. They were all looking at a list on the bulletin board beside the door. Samantha pushed through the boys and ran her finger down the list.

"YYEESSSS!" she cheered. She turned to the others with her hands up in a high-five sign.

One by one, the Clue Club kids slapped

Samantha's hands. "Congratulations, Samantha!" said a couple of the boys who had made the team.

Perry Purple was standing next to Samantha. He looked down the list. When he reached the bottom, he scowled. "Great!" he said, gritting his teeth. "Coach didn't pick me."

"I'm sorry you didn't make it, Perry," said Samantha.

"Yeah, right," said Perry angrily. "It must be a mistake. I should be on the team, not some girl, like you." He turned and stormed up the stairs.

"Whew," said Polly. "Perry is really mad."

"I can't blame him," said Samantha. "I'd be disappointed, too, if I didn't make the team. Listen, I've got to go pick up my sweatshirt. Wait here, guys." She ran into the office.

When Samantha returned, she was carrying a hooded sweatshirt with a number on the back.

"Number one hundred and one," she said proudly. "That's my number."

"That's a good number for you, Samantha," said Wendy. "You gave one hundred and one percent when you tried out for the team."

"Our first practice is tomorrow after school," Samantha said. "Want to come watch?"

"You bet," said Georgie.

"Why don't we go for pizza after the practice?" said Mortimer.

"Great idea! All agreed, say pepperoni!" said Peter.

"PEPPERONI!" they all shouted, then headed home.

The next day, everyone but Samantha was in the library after school getting books for a reading report. Suddenly Wendy pointed out the window to a kid wearing a sweatshirt with 101 on the back. "Look," she whispered to the others. "There's Samantha."

"How can you tell?" asked Mortimer. "I

can't see her face. The sweatshirt hood is up."

"See her number on the back of her sweatshirt?" said Wendy. "Samantha's number one hundred and one."

"I thought Samantha had soccer practice," said Polly. "What's she doing in the schoolyard?"

"Maybe she had to run some laps," said Georgie.

After checking out their books, the kids ran to the soccer field. The field was empty. There was no soccer practice going on.

"Well, here's another mystery," said Wendy. "First we see Samantha where she's not supposed to be. Then we don't see her where she's supposed to be."

"Let's just go to Mama Sophie's and wait for her," said Peter. "We can start on our homework."

"Maybe we'll order a small pizza while we're waiting," said Mortimer.

When Samantha showed up, she explained what had happened.

"After we got dressed, the coach told us the seventh- and eighth-grade soccer team was going to use the soccer field later this afternoon," she told them. "So the junior team practice was moved to the football field on the other side of the school. I didn't have time to come tell you."

"Then what were you doing in the school-yard during practice?" asked Polly.

"We saw you from the library window," Georgie added.

"What? I wasn't at the school," said Samantha. "I was at practice."

"We saw your number on the back of your sweatshirt," said Peter. "Number one-oh-one."

"Well, it wasn't me," said Samantha. "Besides, I can't find my sweatshirt. I thought I put it in my locker, but it's gone."

"Maybe someone took your sweatshirt," said Wendy.

"Nah," said Samantha. "They wouldn't be able to wear it with my number on it. I must have put it somewhere else."

"I gotta go," said Georgie, pushing his chair back. "It's almost four-thirty."

The next day, Principal Higgins called Samantha into his office. When she walked in, Perry Purple was already there. Mr. Higgins held up a sweatshirt with the number 101 on the back. The sweatshirt was covered with dried eggs.

"My soccer sweatshirt!" Samantha gasped. "What happened to it?"

"This was found on school property," Mr. Higgins told her. "And someone threw eggs all over the side of the school yesterday. Perry came in this morning to tell me he saw you doing it."

"Wait a minute, sir," Samantha said. "My friends saw someone in the schoolyard wearing my sweatshirt yesterday. Can you call them in?"

Mr. Higgins asked his secretary to call the Clue Club kids into his office. When they arrived, Mr. Higgins asked Perry to tell his story again.

"I saw Samantha throw some eggs at the school and then run off to the football field for practice," Perry said. "I wasn't going to tell on her at first, but then I decided I should."

Mr. Higgins turned to the Clue Club kids. "Samantha tells me you saw someone running across the schoolyard yesterday wearing her soccer sweatshirt. Is this true?"

"That's right," said Peter. "Samantha said her sweatshirt was missing."

"Samantha didn't lose her sweatshirt," said Perry. "She must have left it by the football field after she threw the eggs."

"What were you doing when you saw Samantha throwing the eggs?" asked Mr. Higgins.

"I was on my way home from school," said Perry.

"Why didn't you tell someone then?" asked Mr. Higgins.

"I had to go straight home from school

yesterday," answered Perry. "I had a dentist appointment."

"I don't think you went straight home, Perry," said Wendy. "In fact, I think you're the one who threw the eggs."

Why does Wendy think Perry threw the eggs at the school?

coach told us about the field change after we got dressed. No one knew before that."

"Perry was in the gym getting Samantha's sweatshirt," said Georgie. "He overheard the coach."

"Well, Perry," said Mr. Higgins. "What do you have to say for yourself?"

"It's not fair," said Perry. "I should be on the soccer team instead of Samantha. She's a girl."

"She's on the team because she's a good player," said Polly.

"You should practice playing soccer instead of lying," said Georgie. "Then you might get on the team."

Solution
The Case of the Soccer Sweatshirt

"What do you mean, Wendy?" asked Mr. Higgins.

"I think Perry took Samantha's sweatshirt. Then he wore it to throw eggs at the school so it would look like Samantha did it," Wendy said.

"Are you sure you're not just trying to help your friend Samantha?" asked Mr. Higgins. "Why are you so sure Perry threw the eggs?"

"Because Perry was so sure Samantha was running back to the football field," answered Wendy.

"Right," said Mortimer. "How did Perry know the practice was at the football field?"

"He couldn't have known that if he went straight home from school," said Polly.

"He knew because he must have been in the gym when the coach told the team," said Peter.

"That's right," said Samantha. "The

2

The Case of the Unforgettable Flag

"What a great day!" cried Polly. "It's too beautiful to be in school."

Polly and the rest of the Clue Club kids stood in the schoolyard, waiting for the morning bell to ring. It was June. School was almost over for the year.

"One more day till the weekend," said Wendy. "I can't wait."

"I can't wait until history class is over," complained Mortimer. "Ms. Redding is going to discuss Flag Day. What a boring holiday."

"Actually, it's more interesting than you think," said Peter. "I was doing a little reading on it last night."

"Peter, everything is interesting to you," laughed Samantha. "As long as you can read up on it."

"Well, Peter, you have to admit, it's def-

16

initely not like Christmas or Halloween, or those fun holidays," said Georgie. "I always forget about Flag Day."

Just then the bell rang, and the kids filed into school. The first class of the day was history.

"Good news, boys and girls," Ms. Redding told her fourth graders. "Today, as you know, is Flag Day. Instead of reading about it in our history books, we have a real historian coming to talk to us about the subject. You all know Mr. Banner, the janitor from the post office. But did you know he is an expert on the U.S. flag? Let's give him a warm welcome."

"Good morning, Mr. Banner," the class said in unison.

"Good morning, everyone," said Mr. Banner. "Thank you for asking me to come and talk about one of my favorite subjects, the flag. Can anyone describe the flag to me?"

Everyone's hand shot up. Georgie was waving excitedly.

"Yes, Georgie," said Mr. Banner.

"It has thirteen stripes," Georgie answered. "Seven red and six white. And there are fifty white stars in a blue rectangle."

"Right," said Mr. Banner. "Now who can tell me what these stars and stripes stand for?"

Not quite as many hands were raised this time. Mr. Banner called on Samantha.

"The thirteen stripes represent the original thirteen colonies," she answered. "And the fifty stars represent the fifty states we have today."

"Good, Samantha," said Mr. Banner. "Anyone know what the red, white, and blue colors represent?"

Peter's hand was the only one up. "White stands for purity. Red represents bravery. And blue stands for justice."

"Excellent!" said Mr. Banner. Then Mr. Banner told the class the history of the American flag from colonial times to the present. Occasionally, he pointed to pictures of old flags he had put on the bulletin board.

When he was finished, Ms. Redding stepped in front of the class. "Did anyone have any idea there was so much to know about the flag?" she asked. "Are there any questions?"

"How did you get so interested in the flag?" asked Mortimer.

Mr. Banner laughed. "It all started when I began working at the post office," he replied. "It's my job to raise and lower the flag each and every day the post office is open. I remembered from Boy Scouts that there were rules on how to do that. So I went to the library and looked them all up before I started my job."

"What are the rules for raising and lowering the flag?" asked Wendy.

"Outside, the flag is usually flown from sunrise to sunset," said Mr. Banner. "But I don't raise the flag exactly at sunrise or lower it at sunset. I raise it first thing when I get to work. And I lower it every night at sunset."

"Mr. Banner, this has been a fascinating history lesson," said Ms. Redding. "Do you agree, class?"

The children all clapped as Mr. Banner nodded and smiled.

After school, the Clue Club kids met on the school playground. They made plans to come back to the school at seven-thirty for Samantha's soccer game.

The game ended around nine o'clock. It was getting dark, but the air was still warm.

"A hot fudge sundae would sure hit the spot," said Georgie.

"I could use a snack, too," agreed Mortimer. "Watching Samantha play so hard made me hungry."

"Everything makes you hungry, Mortimer," laughed Polly.

And with that, the kids headed off down

the main street. The evening sky was clear and the moon was full.

"Look how big the moon is tonight," said Wendy.

"It looks like it's sitting right on top of the post office," said Peter.

When the kids got to the ice-cream parlor, Georgie ordered a hot fudge sundae right away.

"Hmm. There's a Flag Day special," said Mortimer, pointing to a sign in the window. "It's a red, white, and blue sundae. Strawberry and blueberry syrup over vanilla ice cream."

"That sounds great," said Polly. "I think I'll have one of those."

"Wait a minute," said Peter. "We have to go back to the post office. Something is wrong there."

"What are you talking about?" said Georgie.

"Call your father, Wendy," said Peter.

"But why, Peter?" Wendy asked.

"He's the postmaster," Peter said. "So

he has a key to the post office. Call him and tell him to meet us there."

After Wendy called her father, the children raced back to the post office. Just as they reached the front door, Mr. White drove up.

"What's wrong, kids?" he said.

"I think something has happened to Mr. Banner," said Peter.

Why does Peter think something has happened to Mr. Banner?

bered seeing the flag at the post office to-night."

"The flag!" said Wendy. "We saw it flying when we were looking at the moon!"

"Right!" exclaimed Mortimer. "But Mr. Banner is supposed to lower the flag every night before he leaves."

"So he hadn't taken the flag down," said Samantha. "Even though it was after nine o'clock."

"Which meant there might be something wrong," finished Polly.

"Mr. Banner's lucky you kids are such good mystery-solvers," said Mr. White.

"I guess I won't ever forget Flag Day now!" laughed Georgie.

Solution
The Case of the Unforgettable Flag

"You kids wait here," said Mr. White. "I'll go check."

Mr. White searched inside the post office. He found Mr. Banner locked in the basement boiler room.

"I feel pretty foolish," Mr. Banner said, laughing. "I can't believe I locked myself in the boiler room. I've been meaning to fix that lock so this wouldn't happen. Imagine! I go down there a dozen times a day."

The two men walked back to the post office lobby to let the kids know everything was all right. "Don't worry, kids," said Mr. Banner. "My wife would have called Mr. White if I didn't come home."

"How did you know something was wrong?" Mr. White asked Peter.

"It was the Flag Day special sundae that reminded me that Mr. Banner was at school today," said Peter. "Then I remem-

The Case of the Shady Sunglasses

Wendy came running out of her front door when she saw Samantha riding up on her bike. Wendy couldn't wait to tell Samantha the big news.

"I finally saved enough money to buy that pair of blue-tinted sunglasses at the Best View Glasses store," Wendy told her friend quickly. "Want to go with me to get them?"

"Sure," said Samantha. "Get your bike and let's go."

The girls rode to the Best View Glasses store. Wendy ran up to the counter smiling at Mr. Viewmaster, the owner.

"Do you want to look at the glasses again, Wendy?" he asked her.

"No," Wendy replied. "Today I'm a customer!" She began counting out her money.

"Do you want me to put these in a bag or will you wear them?" laughed Mr. Viewmaster.

"What do you think?" said Wendy, putting on the glasses.

"Super!" said Samantha.

"You got them just in time," Mr. Viewmaster told her. "You just bought the last pair of these we have. This style has been discontinued and we won't be getting any more in."

"You were meant to have those glasses, Wendy," laughed Samantha.

The next day was the last day of school. Wendy wore her sunglasses into Ms. Redding's classroom.

"Wendy, we're not out of school for another half hour," said Ms. Redding. "Do you mind waiting until then to wear your sunglasses?"

"Oh, sorry," smiled Wendy, removing the glasses.

Outside on the playground, Suzie Salmon tried the glasses on. "Do you care if I get a pair just like them?" she asked Wendy. "I'm leaving for camp tomorrow and I need some."

"I don't care, but there aren't any more like them," Wendy told her. "Mr. Viewmaster told me this style has been discontinued."

"You wouldn't sell yours to me, would you?" Suzie asked.

"Are you kidding?" laughed Wendy. "I saved my allowance for three weeks to buy these glasses. I love them!"

Two weeks later, the Clue Club was having their Saturday meeting in Wendy's backyard. Wendy decided to have the meeting outside so she could wear her sunglasses.

"You've turned into a big-time movie star, Wendy," Peter kidded her. "You haven't taken your sunglasses off in two weeks."

After the meeting, the kids went into the house to get drinks and some lunch before playing Clue Jr. outside. Wendy left her sunglasses on the lawn chair and when she returned, they were gone.

"Now what did I do with my sunglasses?" Wendy asked the others. "I must have put them down inside when I had lunch." The kids helped her look inside the house, and outside, too, but her glasses were nowhere to be found.

On Monday everyone met at Wendy's house again before going to a movie. Just as they were ready to leave, Mrs. White called up the stairs. "Wendy, I have something for you."

"Did you find my sunglasses?" Wendy exclaimed, running down the stairs to her mother.

"No, honey," her mom answered. "I'm afraid not. It's a postcard from Suzie Salmon."

Wendy showed the postcard to the rest

of the kids who had followed her downstairs. On one side of the card was a picture of the camp.

"Oh," cried Wendy. "The date of the postcard is the same awful day I lost my sunglasses."

"Look at the cool stamp," said Mortimer. "Can I have it for my collection? It's not all messed up."

"Sure," said Wendy. "We'll steam it off later. Right now we better hurry or we'll be late for the movie." She shoved the postcard in her bag as she and the rest of the kids rushed out the door.

The next week, the Clue Club kids were at a pool party given by one of their friends from school.

"Look," Samantha said to Wendy. "There's Suzie with a pair of sunglasses just like the ones you lost." The Clue Club kids walked over to Suzie.

"I see you got a pair of those cool sunglasses, Suzie," Wendy said.

"Yeah," Suzie answered. "You know I

wanted those glasses ever since I saw you wearing them. And I finally got a pair at Best View yesterday."

"That's funny," said Wendy. "Mr. Viewmaster told me my glasses were the last pair in the store."

"So where are your glasses?" asked Suzie.

"I don't know," answered Wendy. "They disappeared."

"You wouldn't know anything about Wendy's lost glasses, would you, Suzie?" said Georgie.

"Don't look at me, Georgie," Suzie snapped. "I didn't take them. I was at swimming camp right after school got out. Didn't you get my postcard, Wendy? I sent you one from camp. There's a date on the card that proves I was at camp when you lost your sunglasses."

"Yes, I got your card," said Wendy. "In fact, I think it's still in my bag." She showed the postcard to the rest of the Clue Club.

"See?" said Wendy. "The date is the same day I lost my glasses."

"Well, I hate to say this," said Polly. "But I don't think you were at swimming camp when Wendy's sunglasses disappeared. I don't think you are telling the truth, Suzie."

Why does Polly think Suzie isn't telling the truth about when she was at camp?

put the exact date you stole Wendy's sunglasses on your card, then you put it in her mailbox yourself a few days later. You had to because you were already home from camp."

Suzie was embarrassed to be caught in a lie in front of all her friends. She gave the sunglasses back and apologized to Wendy.

Georgie held up a mirror for Wendy. "Take a good look, Wendy," he said.

"I'm just glad Polly took a good look at that postcard," smiled Wendy.

Solution
The Case of the Shady Sunglasses

"What do you mean?" said Suzie.

"Well, Suzie, let's just say your postcard is a phony," said Polly. "For one thing, why are you so sure the date on your postcard is the date Wendy's sunglasses disappeared?"

"That's right," said Peter. "No one said exactly when the sunglasses disappeared."

"How would you know, unless you took them?" said Georgie.

"So what?" said Suzie. "It was a lucky guess. But the postcard still proves I was at camp when they were lost."

"No, it doesn't," said Samantha. "Look closely. Something's missing on that card."

"Hey! There's no postmark on the stamp," said Mortimer. "I never thought of that when I asked if I could have it for my stamp collection. Suzie never mailed the card."

"That's what I think," said Polly. "You

4

The Case of the Disappearing Footprints

Samantha, Mortimer, Georgie, and Wendy were all standing in front of Polly Peacock's house. Beside them were a pile of surfboards, beach balls, and rubber rafts. Polly's parents were taking the Clue Club kids to their beach house for a couple of days. Meanwhile, everyone was waiting for Peter Plum.

"The car is almost packed," Mr. Peacock said. "We'll give Peter a couple more minutes, then we'll swing by his house and pick him up."

"Wonder why Peter is late this time," said Samantha. Peter was always late.

"He was probably *just reading up* on something and lost track of time," said Wendy. Everyone chuckled. Peter was always saying, "I was just reading up on something."

"I can't believe he would be late today," said Mortimer. "I don't want to miss even a minute at the beach."

Just then, Peter came running up the block. "Sorry to be late," he panted. "I was just reading up on . . ." Everyone burst into laughter.

"Never mind, Peter," said Mrs. Peacock, shaking her head. "It doesn't matter. Just throw your bag into the back of the van and we'll be off."

After they arrived at the beach and unpacked their things, Polly said, "Come on, everybody. I want you to see my favorite place here. It's called Point Rock."

The kids hiked down the beach for about half a mile.

"Where is this place?" asked Mortimer. "Are we almost there?"

"It's just around that bend," said Polly, pointing ahead. As soon as the kids turned the bend, they saw a huge rock that jutted out into the water.

"There it is!" cried Polly. "Point Rock."

"Wow!" said Georgie. "It was worth the walk."

"Look how smooth the beach is here," said Wendy, pointing down at the sand.

"Yeah, except for all the little bird tracks," said Peter.

"No one comes up here very often," Polly said. "Sometimes the seagulls have this beach all to themselves."

The kids climbed the massive rock and sat on top for a while until Polly said they should leave. "The tide is coming in," she explained.

"That's what I was reading up on this morning — tides," said Peter. "I thought since we were going to be at the beach for a couple of days, we'd be able to see the tide go in and out."

"You will," said Polly. "But for now, let's get off Point Rock so we can watch it and not get wet."

They climbed down and sat up on the beach to watch the tide come in. Before long, the water had surrounded Point Rock until it looked like an island. Walking back to the house, the kids saw their footprints disappear in the foam behind them.

Georgie was amazed that the tide came in so far. "Look how deep the water is getting around Point Rock!" he exclaimed.

"Soon there won't be any way to get to Point Rock," said Polly, "except by swimming."

"Speaking of swimming," said Mortimer, "I want to try out my new surfboard. The waves look perfect!"

On the way back, Peter talked about how tides go in and out at different times each day and how they are affected by the moon's gravity. When they got back to the beach house, they saw a boy sitting on the porch next door.

"Hey, Barry!" called Polly, running up

to him. "Long time, no see." Polly introduced Barry Brown to the Clue Club. "His parents own the beach house next to ours," Polly explained.

"Hi, Barry," everyone said.

"What's wrong, Barry?" asked Peter. "You don't look too happy."

"My boogie board is missing," Barry told them. "But I saw the kid who ran off with it. He was wearing a blue bathing suit with red surfboards on it."

"Let's check around and see if there are any clues," said Samantha.

When the Clue Club walked around the house, they discovered a kid leaning the boogie board up against the back porch. He was wearing a blue bathing suit with red surfboards on it.

"Hey!" Barry yelled. "What are you doing with my boogie board?"

"Calm down. I'm Fred Flora from down the street," the kid told Barry. "I was just returning your boogie board."

"Why were you leaving it in back of the house?" asked Barry.

"I'm really late for lunch and my mom's going to be mad," Fred explained. "I saw the board on the beach and was just returning it."

"How did you know it was mine?" asked Barry.

"I've seen you with it," said Fred.

"How do I know you didn't take it this morning?" asked Barry.

"I couldn't have," said Fred. "I went up to Point Rock early today. I like to climb up to the very top and just hang out."

"We climbed up Point Rock today and we didn't see you," said Mortimer.

"Yeah, well, I went up there real early this morning," said Fred. "But I didn't stay long. I walked on down the beach to Point Sandy. I saw your boogie board on the beach when I was coming back. So I grabbed it for you."

"I think you grabbed it all right," said

Samantha. "But not just now. You grabbed it this morning."

Why does Samantha think Fred took Barry's boogie board?

didn't take the boogie board. I only borrowed it. See? I'm returning it now."

"You should have asked me first," said Barry.

"That's right. Something else is missing besides your footprints," said Georgie. "Your manners."

Solution
The Case of the Disappearing
Footprints

"How do you know he took the board?" asked Barry.

"Because he's lying about being at Point Rock this morning," said Samantha.

"What?" said Fred. "How can you say that?"

"Because your footprints were missing," said Samantha.

"That's right," said Peter. "There were no footprints in the sand when we went there. The beach was smooth."

"No one had walked on the beach this morning," said Mortimer.

"Maybe I walked there after you guys left," said Fred.

"No way," said Polly. "The tide came in as we were leaving."

"So no one could have walked to Point Rock after that," said Wendy.

"I'm not lying," said Fred stubbornly. "I

5

The Case of the Blackberry Pie

It was the middle of July. Mortimer's family had just gotten back from vacation and the Clue Club was having its weekly Saturday meeting at his house.

"You picked a good week to be gone," Polly told Mortimer. "It's been raining for a week."

"But the rain is supposed to stop this afternoon," said Wendy. "And the weather announcer says it will be sunny and hot tomorrow."

"Let's go swimming at Fish Fin Lake tomorrow afternoon," said Georgie.

"Yeah," said Peter Plum. "We can play Clue Jr. and have a picnic, too."

"Everyone can bring something to eat or drink," said Samantha.

"Mmm," said Mortimer mysteriously. "I know what I'll bring."

The next day, when the kids unpacked their picnic offerings, Mortimer took out a whole blackberry pie.

"Oh," exclaimed Polly. "It's still warm!"

"My mom baked it this morning," said Mortimer. "I picked the blackberries myself," he added proudly.

"Where did you pick them?" asked Peter. "Did you get them here at the lake?"

"Where?" asked Samantha. "There are blackberries around here?"

"Yeah," said Peter. "You know that gully beyond the woods behind the lake? There's a whole patch of blackberry bushes in the gully."

"I didn't know that," said Wendy.

"Me, either," Mort said. "But I picked these when we were on vacation last week. Then we froze them. One day my whole family went berry picking. At first I didn't want to do it because the bushes were full of thorns. But my mom said I would appreciate my food more if I had to work a little to get it."

"Well?" asked Samantha.

"I hate to say it, but she was right," admitted Mortimer. "Picking the berries was a super hassle. The bushes are real thick. I wore long pants and socks to protect my legs when we walked through them. And my hands got all scratched up, no matter how careful I was. Not to mention all the purple berry stains. But it was worth it. I picked enough for three pies — all by myself. We already had one last night. I thought I'd share one with you guys."

Just then Paula Periwinkle, Gwen Garnet, Connie Cardinal, and June Jade walked over to say hi.

"What kind of pie is that, Mortimer?" Gwen asked.

"Blackberry," answered Mortimer.

"And he picked the berries himself," said Wendy.

"Mmm," said Paula. "Can we have some?"

"Sorry," Mortimer replied. "I promised all of this one to the Clue Club."

"And it's a promise I hope he keeps," said Georgie.

"Okay, okay," June laughed. "We understand."

"Well, we'll see you guys later," said Paula.

"Let's go for a swim," said Samantha. "It's really hot."

"Race you to the dock," shouted Georgie. And the kids all plunged into the cool lake.

A half hour later, they were hungry and decided to get out and eat. When they reached the shore, Samantha called out, "Race you to the pie!"

Polly looked down at the mud along the lake's edge. "My feet are going to get dirty," she said. "I don't want to get my blanket all muddy."

"What can you expect, Polly?" laughed Peter. "It's been raining for days. You can keep your blanket clean. Just don't step on it."

When the kids reached their spot, they found half the blackberry pie had been eaten.

"Someone ate the blackberry pie!" cried Mortimer angrily.

Just then Paula, Gwen, Connie, and June ran past them toward the lake.

"Hey, look!" cried Georgie. "They have purple stains all over their faces and hands."

"I'll bet those girls ate my pie," said Mortimer.

"Well, let's ask them right now," said Samantha. "Come on." The kids caught up to the girls before they jumped into the water.

"What happened to you?" asked Polly.

"How come you have purple stains all over your face?"

"Oh, uh, we just had some grape ice-pops," explained Paula.

"Yeah, we're going in to wash it off," said Connie.

"Those aren't ice-pop stains," shouted Mortimer. "I can see parts of berries."

"Tell the truth. How did you guys get those purple stains?" asked Georgie.

"Well," began Gwen. "It's true they are blackberry stains. But we didn't eat Mortimer's pie."

"No," said Paula. "We picked some berries ourselves in the berry patch behind the lake."

"That's right," said June. "Seeing your pie gave us the idea to go there and pick some ourselves."

"We picked a lot, too," said Connie.

"We cleaned off several bushes," said Paula. "And we ate them all!"

"I don't know if you ate my pie," said

Mortimer. "But I'm sure you didn't pick any blackberries."

How does Mortimer know the girls didn't pick blackberries?

mer told us about all the clothes he had to wear to keep from getting scratched by the blackberry thorns."

"There's no way you could have picked blackberries in your bathing suits," said Peter. "Your legs and arms would be all scratched up."

"You're right," said Gwen. "But we only ate half the pie. You still have the rest."

"I'm sorry, Mortimer," said Paula. "It just looked so good."

"Well, next time pick your own berries," said Mortimer.

"This sure was a thorny case," said Georgie, as the kids finished off the pie.

"Yes, but it has a sweet ending," laughed Mortimer.

Solution
The Case of the Blackberry Pie

"What do you mean, we didn't pick any berries?" said Paula. "I told you, we walked over to the gully behind the lake. There are a whole bunch of blackberry bushes there."

"Yeah," said June. "Why do you say that, Mortimer?"

"Because you're too clean," said Mortimer.

"Too clean?" exclaimed Connie. "But we have purple stains all over us."

"That's not the kind of clean I mean," said Mortimer.

"I get it," said Polly. "They aren't muddy."

"And they would be really muddy if they had been tromping around in the woods," said Georgie.

"And they're not scratched up," said Wendy.

"That's right," said Samantha. "Morti-

The Case of the Vanishing Prize

It was after school on Friday. The Clue Club kids met on the playground to discuss what they were going to do on the long weekend coming up. School would be closed for Columbus Day, and the stores in town were celebrating with special events.

"What a great weekend!" exclaimed Peter. "It starts off with our Clue Club meeting Saturday morning at my house. And I have a surprise planned."

"Then Sunday afternoon we help Mama Sophie clean up the pizza parlor for her Columbus Day special," said Samantha.

"Yeah," said Mortimer. "She's giving away free pizza to everyone who helps her. Every kid in town will be there cleaning."

"Plus her pizzas are half price on Monday," said Polly. "Since she's Italian, she goes all out on Columbus Day."

"And all the downtown stores are having drawings for prizes," said Wendy.

"Best of all, Monday is a holiday," said Georgie. "No school!"

The next day, Peter served the Clue Club Italian pastries for a snack in honor of Columbus Day. "My mom got them at an Italian bakery in Hobart," he told the others. "These things that look like icing in a tube are called cannoli. They're my favorites."

"Mmm," said Georgie. "There should be more Italian holidays. Today we're having pastries and tomorrow we eat free pizza."

The next afternoon the kids headed to Mama Sophie's Pizza Parlor. The place was full of kids washing windows, wiping off counters and tables, and scrubbing floors and walls. Mama's son, Tonio, was blowing up balloons that said VIVA ITALY! on them.

Later that afternoon, Mama served up pizza to her hungry crew.

"Don't forget now," Mama told everybody. "Tomorrow, the pizza is half price in honor of the great Italian explorer Christopher Columbus."

"Don't worry," said Mortimer, taking a third slice of pizza from a tray. "No kid forgets half-priced pizza."

"Let's go to Blueville's sporting goods store," said Wendy. "I want to put my name in for the mountain bike drawing."

"Me, too," said Samantha.

"I'd love to win that," said Georgie.

"Best View Glasses is having a drawing for those cool wrap sunglasses we tried on last week," Polly said to Mortimer.

"The computer store and the sneaker store are giving away prizes, too," said Mortimer.

"Well, let's go check out all the prizes," said Peter.

The kids visited all the stores to enter their drawing slips. On their way to the sporting goods store they passed by Mama Sophie's.

"Look!" said Polly. "Tonio's finished decorating the outside."

"Wow!" exclaimed Samantha. "Look at all the balloons floating above the store sign."

"There must be a hundred," said Wendy.

Inside the sporting goods store, Mr. Blueville and Officer Lawford were talking to Ralph Ruby. Ralph had been nicknamed Red because of his red hair. Mr. Blueville claimed he saw Red ride off on the mountain bike that was set up outside as a display.

"You're sure it was Red?" Officer Lawford asked him.

"I didn't get a look at his face," admitted Mr. Blueville. "But I saw his red hair."

"That's not fair," said Ralph. "Other kids in town have red hair. Besides, I've been over at the pizza parlor helping clean all afternoon."

"Were you kids at the pizza parlor?" Officer Lawford asked the Clue Club.

"Yes, sir," answered Peter.

"I bet every kid in town was," said Georgie.

"Did you see Red there?" asked Officer Lawford.

"I think I saw him outside when we left," said Wendy. "But I don't know about before."

Officer Lawford called Mama Sophie on the phone and asked her if Red was there helping. "I think so," Mama told him. "But there were so many kids here cleaning, I can't remember exactly."

"Sure, I was there," insisted Ralph. "I was blowing up balloons all afternoon. They used them to decorate the front of the store. I blew up so many balloons, I don't have enough breath left to ride a bicycle."

"Well, we'll have to question the other boys in town with red hair," Officer Lawford told Mr. Blueville. "In the meantime, you can go, Red."

"Excuse me, Officer Lawford," said Georgie. "But Red's story has as much hot air as a hot-air balloon."

Why does Georgie think Red is lying?

Solution
The Case of the Vanishing Prize

"What do you mean?" asked Officer Lawford.

"I mean Red is lying about helping at the pizza store," said Georgie. "At least, he never blew up any balloons."

"That's right," said Wendy. "Tonio was blowing up the balloons with a tank of helium."

"That's why they were floating high above the pizza parlor sign," said Peter.

"If you didn't know the balloons were helium, that means you weren't at the pizza parlor," said Mortimer.

"Which means you weren't there all afternoon helping to clean," said Samantha.

"Which means you could have been here taking the bike," finished Polly.

"What about it?" said Officer Lawford. "Tell us the truth, son."

"I just wanted to see how a mountain

bike felt to ride," Red told Mr. Blueville. "I was going to bring it back tomorrow for the drawing."

"Well, suppose we go get it right now," said Officer Lawford.

"Since you didn't blow up any balloons, I guess you have enough breath to ride it back to the store," said Georgie.

The Case of the Lucky Hockey Wheels

As soon as Georgie's parents brought him home from the store, he called up his friend Peter.

"Peter, come over and see the new hockey wheels I just got for my in-line skates," said Georgie.

"Cool!" said Peter. "Just in time for the neighborhood hockey game tomorrow. I'll be right over."

Peter called the rest of the Clue Club. In no time, Wendy, Samantha, Mortimer, and Polly all skated over to Georgie's to check out his new wheels. When they got to Georgie's house, Georgie was in the garage painting a tiny star design on the sides of the wheels.

"What are you doing, Georgie?" asked Wendy.

"I am putting my good luck mark on my new wheels," said Georgie. "Isn't it cool? My new wheels are the best."

Georgie put the wheels on his skates with the designs facing in. Then the kids skated over to the school's outdoor basketball court, where the hockey game was going to be held. They wanted to watch Georgie try out his new wheels. On the way, they accidentally skated over a freshly tarred section of the school parking lot.

"Your new wheels!" said Polly. "They were so white. Now they're all black on the bottom.

"Oh, well," said Georgie. "Maybe that will bring me more luck in the hockey game tomorrow."

At the basketball court, Georgie showed his new wheels to several other kids who were planning to skate in the game. Some of the boys wouldn't be able to play because they didn't have hockey wheels.

"The only wheels I have are super-lights," D.J. Dark said. "They're good for street skating and jumping. But playing hockey on the hard concrete would chip them."

"I know what you mean," said Greg Grape. "I just got some new midgets. Boy, are those wheels expensive — too expensive to ruin playing hockey. Forget it! They'd chip, too."

"Tell me about it!" agreed Billy Blond. "I got some for my birthday, but I had to choose between midgets or hockey wheels. My parents said they cost too much for me to get both."

"Yeah, I had to mow the grass for two months to earn enough for my hockey wheels," said Georgie. "Listen, I'll see you later, guys. I'm gonna repack my bearings so the wheels are extra fast."

"I gotta go, too," said Samantha. "It's getting late."

"Yeah, it's almost time to eat dinner," said Mortimer.

"Mortimer, you always think it's time to

eat," Polly said. "Come on, I'll race you home."

"Yeah, I told my folks I'd be home in a half hour," said Peter.

When Georgie got to his garage, he took off his new hockey wheels. He began carefully putting fresh grease in the wheel bearings. Georgie was about to put the wheels back on, but his father called him to supper. After dinner, Georgie went back out to the garage. His skates were there, but his hockey wheels were gone.

Georgie called Peter on the phone right away. "Can you believe it?" he told Peter. "I left the garage door open when I went inside for dinner. Someone took my new hockey wheels while I was eating. It must have been someone who knew that I was going to take my wheels off."

"That's a lot of kids," said Peter. "You told everyone at the basketball court that today you were going to repack your bearings."

"The only other wheels I have will chip on the hard concrete," wailed Georgie. "I guess I'm out of the game."

The next day, Georgie and Peter skated over to the basketball court. They met up with the rest of the Clue Club to watch the hockey game.

"Gee, half the school is here," said Samantha.

"And half of them are skating," sighed Georgie. "I wish I was."

"Georgie, why aren't you skating?" asked Wendy.

"Yeah," said Polly. "Why do you have on your old wheels?"

"Because someone took my new hockey wheels out of my garage while I was repacking the bearings last night," Georgie muttered.

Georgie watched everyone skating around in a circle on the court. When D.J. Dark skated by, Georgie called out to him, "Hey, D.J." D.J. skated over to Georgie.

"I thought you weren't able to play," Georgie said. "You said you didn't have hockey wheels."

"Guess what! My parents got me these new awesome hockey wheels this morning," said D.J. "My parents were saving the wheels for the hockey game today. I just put them on."

He held up his foot so that Georgie could admire his new wheels.

Just then Billy Blond skated by. "Hi, Georgie," he called out.

"Billy, are you skating, too?" said Georgie.

"I borrowed my brother's skates," said Billy. "They're a little too big, but I put on three pairs of socks."

"How come you're not skating, Georgie?" asked D.J.

"As if you didn't know, D.J.," said Peter, looking at D.J.'s wheels.

"What are you talking about, Peter?" said D.J.

"You know Georgie's not skating be-

cause someone took his new hockey wheels," said Peter.

"How should I know that?" said D.J.

"Because I think that you took them," said Peter.

Why does Peter think D.J. Dark took Georgie's new hockey wheels?

Solution
The Case of the Lucky Hockey Wheels

"What are you talking about?" said D.J.

"You have them on your skates," said Peter.

"Forget it," said D.J. "All hockey wheels look alike."

"Georgie's were special," said Samantha. "He painted his good luck charm on them." She pointed to one of the wheels. "It looks just like the design on that wheel."

"It's . . . it's just the wheel company's logo," D.J. stammered.

"And," continued Polly. "There was something else special about Georgie's wheels."

"They were dirty," added Mortimer.

"That makes them special?" said D.J. "All hockey wheels are dirty."

"Not brand-new ones, like yours," said Wendy. "They don't get that dirty so fast."

"Look at the bottoms of your wheels," said Polly. "Yuk."

"Let me see your skates again," said Georgie. "That's my good luck charm, all right." He reached down and touched the bottom of D.J.'s wheel. "It's tar," he shouted. "Black tar that I skated through yesterday! These are my wheels!"

"Well, D.J., it looks like you won't be skating in the hockey game after all," said Peter.

"No, but *I* will," exclaimed Georgie. "Take those off, D.J. I'm going to put those wheels on the right skates!"

"You were right about those marks being good luck, Georgie," said Mortimer.

The Case of the Runaway Turtle

Don't you think that this is the best science project Ms. Redding has ever come up with?" Peter asked his friends.

Mortimer, Samantha, Wendy, and Georgie all nodded their heads. Even Polly was grinning, and science was not her favorite subject.

"This project makes me even like science!" said Polly. "I especially like the part about being able to bring our pets into school."

Ms. Redding's science project was called "My Mystery Pet." Some of her fourth-grade students were bringing their pets to school. But they also had to find out a little-known fact about the animal to share with the class.

Polly and Peter were working on the project together. They had asked the Clue Club kids to come over to Peter's so they could practice their question on them. When the other kids arrived, Peter and Polly took them around to the back-yard. Peter's dog Bizzy jumped up to lick everyone's hands. On the picnic table sat a small wooden box with a wire lid over it.

"Oooh," said Samantha, lifting off the wire lid. "It's Speedo!"

"Yes," said Polly, picking up her pet tur-tle. "Peter and I are going to use Speedo and Bizzy for our project."

"Here's our mystery question," said Peter. He held up a sign that read, WHAT IS SOMETHING BOTH OUR PETS ENJOY DOING?

"Can you guess what it is?" asked Peter, hopping up and down with excitement. The other kids looked at each other and shrugged. No one could come up with any-thing.

"Looks like we've stumped them, Peter," Polly said, grinning.

"All right, guys, we'll give you a clue," Peter said. He ran to the shed and grabbed a dog biscuit from a box just inside the door.

When Peter held up the dog biscuit, Bizzy stood on his hind legs and walked across the yard to get it. After the kids finished clapping for Bizzy, Polly put Speedo at one end of the picnic table and held out another dog biscuit. Speedo crawled over to the biscuit and ate it out of Polly's hand.

"They both like eating dog food?" she asked.

"Yes!" said Polly.

"I never knew that," said Wendy.

"There are a lot of other neat things about turtles," said Polly. "Some of them, like Speedo, are even attracted to the color red."

"Wow," said Georgie. "I thought turtles were just lumps that sat around in their bowls."

"Most people do, but I know that is not true," said Polly proudly.

"All this talk about biscuits has made me hungry," said Mortimer. "How about some lunch?"

"My mom said she'd make us some sandwiches," said Peter. "Let's go see what she made us for lunch."

Polly put Speedo back into his box and set the box on the table. Halfway to the house, she looked at the shade tree beside the picnic table and ran back.

"Anything wrong?" asked Wendy when Polly came into the house.

"No. I wanted to move Speedo's box out of the shade," Polly told the others. "He needs to sit in the sun to keep warm. If he gets too cool, he'll get sleepy and forget to eat."

After lunch, the Clue Club kids headed outside again to play a game of Clue Jr. under the tree.

"Oh, no," cried Polly. "Speedo's box is on the ground."

Mortimer ran over to the table. "Not only that, but the wire lid is off and Speedo is gone," said Mortimer.

"How did this happen?" Polly cried. "Where's Speedo?"

"I guess this is my fault," said Georgie, hanging his head. "I came outside while everyone was still eating. I wanted to see if Speedo would come to me if I held out a dog biscuit. I guess I forgot to put the box back on the table."

"I guess you forgot to put the lid back on tight, too," said Polly angrily. "Speedo has gotten out of his box."

"I'm really sorry, Polly," said Georgie. "I'll help you look for him."

"Don't worry, Polly, we'll find him," said Peter.

"Look, aren't those turtle tracks, Polly?" said Samantha. She pointed to Speedo's tracks leading across the dirt toward the shed.

"They are!" exclaimed Polly. "Let's follow them."

The kids followed the tracks until they disappeared just inside the shed.

"Maybe Speedo is behind something in the shed," said Wendy.

"Let's get busy looking before Speedo speeds away," said Mortimer. The kids looked all around the shed, but there was no Speedo to be seen.

"Maybe we should look outside the shed," said Peter. "It doesn't look like Speedo's in here."

"Oh, my poor Speedo," wailed Polly. "Where are you?"

"Come on, guys," said Georgie. "We're the Clue Club. We can solve this mystery. Let's check again."

"I think he's in the shed, said Samantha. "Since there are no tracks coming out, he must still be in there."

"I think you're right," said Peter. "Let's look around the shed again."

After a moment of looking around, Samantha's face suddenly lit up. "Wait a min-

ute, guys," she said. "I think I know where Speedo went."

"You do?" exclaimed Polly. "Where, Samantha?"

"I'll give you a clue," said Samantha. "Speedo is in the shed, right where the tracks led us."

Where does Samantha think Speedo is?

Solution
The Case of the Runaway Turtle

"But we looked everywhere in the shed," said Mortimer.

"We looked *behind* everything," said Samantha. "But not *in* everything." Samantha pointed toward the shed door. The kids turned around to look.

"That's it!" cried Wendy, pointing to a box of dog biscuits lying on the floor. The box had fallen over and the lid was open. "You think Speedo is in the box of dog food?"

Polly ran to the box, knelt down, and peered inside. Sure enough, there was her turtle, fast asleep.

"Ssssssh," whispered Polly. "Speedo's asleep."

"Now I remember," said Georgie. "Speedo likes dog food."

"He must have crawled inside the box to have a treat," said Wendy.

"Then he fell asleep in the box because

he wasn't in the warm sun," said Peter.

"That's right," said Mortimer. "Polly said Speedo would get sleepy if he got cool."

"Good work, Samantha," said Wendy.

"That's right," said Georgie. "Speedo was saved by the biscuit."

Your favorite game is a mystery series!

Clue Jr.™

created by
Parker C. Hinter

Samantha Scarlet, Peter Plum, and Mortimer Mustard need your help! If you like playing the game Clue® Jr., you'll love helping the Clue® Jr. Kids solve the mysteries in these great books!

☐ BBJ47907-5 **#1 The Case of the Secret Message** **$2.95**
☐ BBJ47908-3 **#2 The Case of the Stolen Jewel** **$2.99**
☐ BBJ26217-3 **#3 The Case of the**
Chocolate Fingerprints **$2.99**
☐ BBJ26218-1 **#4 The Case of the Missing Movie** **$2.99**
☐ BBJ62372-9 **#5 The Case of the Zoo Clue** **$2.99**

Available wherever you buy books...or use this order form

- -

Scholastic Inc., P.O. Box 7502, 2931 E. McCarty Street, Jefferson City, MO 65102-7502

Please send me the books I have checked above. I am enclosing $_____
(please add $2.00 to cover shipping and handling). Send check or money order —
no cash or C.O.D.s please.

Name_____ **Birthdate** _____

Address _____

City_____ **State/Zip** _____

Please allow four to six weeks for delivery. Offer good in the U.S. only. Sorry, mail orders are not available to residents of Canada. Prices subject to change.

CLJR795

8.04